NOV - - 2023

HEIDI HECKELBECK

The Secret's Out!

By Wanda Coven
Illustrated by Priscilla Burris

LITTLE SIMON
New York London Toronto Sydney New Delhi

LITTLE SIMON
An imprint of Simon & Schuster Children's Publishing Division
1230 Avenue of the Americas, New York, New York 10020
First Little Simon paperback edition September 2023
Copyright © 2023 by Simon & Schuster, Inc.
Also available in a Little Simon hardcover edition.
All rights reserved, including the right of reproduction in whole or in part in any form. LITTLE SIMON is a registered trademark of Simon & Schuster, Inc., and associated colophon is a trademark of Simon & Schuster, Inc. For information about special discounts for bulk purchases, please contact Simon & Schuster Special Sales at 1-866-506-1949 or business@simonandschuster.com.
The Simon & Schuster Speakers Bureau can bring authors to your live event. For more information or to book an event contact the Simon & Schuster Speakers Bureau at 1-866-248-3049 or visit our website at www.simonspeakers.com.
Designed by Ciara Gay and Chrisila Maida
Manufactured in the United States of America 0823 LAK
10 9 8 7 6 5 4 3 2 1
Library of Congress Cataloging-in-Publication Data
Names: Coven, Wanda, author. | Burris, Priscilla, illustrator.
Title: Heidi Heckelbeck the secret's out / by Wanda Coven ; illustrated by Priscilla Burris.
Other titles: Secret's out
Description: First Little Simon paperback edition. | New York : Little Simon, 2023. | Series: Heidi Heckelbeck ; 36 | Summary: When Heidi's magic unexpectedly transfers to her best friend Lucy, Heidi reveals her secret in an effort to get it back.
Identifiers: LCCN 2023006637 (print) | LCCN 2023006638 (ebook) | ISBN 9781665911344 (paperback) | ISBN 9781665911351 (hardcover) | ISBN 9781665911368 (ebook)
Subjects: CYAC: Witches—Fiction. | Magic—Fiction. | Secrets—Fiction. | Best friends—Fiction. | Friendship—Fiction.
Classification: LCC PZ7.C83393 Hr 2023 (print) | LCC PZ7.C83393 (ebook) | DDC [Fic]—dc23
LC record available at https://lccn.loc.gov/2023006637
LC ebook record available at https://lccn.loc.gov/2023006638

CONTENTS

Chapter 1

A PERFECT START

Heidi woke up *before* her alarm *and* before Mom could pop in to say, "Wake up, buttercup!"

Heidi even woke up before her little brother, Henry.

She hopped out of bed and glanced in the mirror.

Wow, my hair looks salon PERFECT! she thought. *I'm off to a great start!* Then Heidi grabbed her totally already-packed backpack. As soon as she stepped into the hall, she stopped.

"*Mmm,*" she murmured, taking a deep breath. "Something smells AMAZING!"

Heidi clumped downstairs to the kitchen as fast as she could. Dad had made his famous salted dark-chocolate waffles.

"It's not even Saturday!" Heidi exclaimed as she picked two perfect waffles.

She sat at the table and sighed happily.

"I think this may be the PERFECT day!" Heidi cheered.

Dad pulled a waffle off the iron with a fork. "Well, don't jinx it!" he said.

"That's funny," said Mom. "I'm having a perfect day too! I just found my lost bracelet. It's been missing for over a year! Can you believe it?"

Mom jangled her bracelet. The little bell that hung from it jingled.

Dad pointed to Henry's empty seat at the table and said, "Hmm, we seem to be missing someone if this day is going to be perfect. Heidi, can you please wake up your sleepyhead brother?"

Heidi shoveled another bite into her mouth and nodded. She liked being the waker-upper rather than the one being woken up.

Heidi ran upstairs and opened Henry's door.

"Hey, Henry!" she whispered. "It's time to get up!"

Henry jumped up from bed and flopped like a fish out of water.

"Don't WHISPER!" Henry said. "I thought you were a GHOST!"

Heidi giggled and rolled her eyes. "Get up before you miss the bus," she said. "Oh, and PS, I'm pretty sure there are no such things as ghosts."

Henry covered his head with a pillow. "You're only PRETTY sure?" he asked.

Heidi laughed. "Well, you never know with ghosts," she said, shutting the door behind her.

Then she opened the door back up and cried, *"BOO!"*

Chapter 2

LOLLiPOP SECRETS

Why is Bruce Bickerson sitting next to a kindergartner? Heidi wondered as she boarded the bus. Where was she supposed to sit now?

"Sit here," someone said.

It was Stanley Stonewrecker, and he slapped the empty seat beside him.

So Heidi happily slid onto the seat beside Stanley. Now her perfect day was back on track.

"What's up, cool pup?" she asked.

Stanley let out a big laugh and said, "Wow, you're in a good mood!"

Heidi bounced on the seat. "I'm having the perfect day!" she told him.

"Cool, but this might make it better," said Stanley as he pulled a lollipop from his backpack.

Heidi squealed. Every kid knew that lollipops made everything better.

Heidi read the wrapper. "Candy Pop: Grape. I've seen this kind of lollipop before! Remember when we were partners for the science fair?"

"Um, how could I forget?" said Stanley. "Melanie and Bruce's volcano erupted all over the judges . . . AND MELANIE! But what does the science fair have to do with lollipops?"

"BECAUSE I had a secret admirer then," said Heidi. "And they gave me grape Candy Pops just like this!"

Stanley's face suddenly became red and blotchy.

"Is something wrong?" asked Heidi.

Stanley rubbed his red cheeks and said, "Well, um, those lollipops were from ME, Heidi."

Heidi's eyes went wide as she said, "NO WAY! From YOU? Why didn't you ever tell me?"

Stanley shrugged. "I guess I chickened out. But I won't now. Maybe . . . we could hang out . . . sometime . . . together—unless you don't want to or anything. It's cool."

Heidi couldn't believe her ears!

"I'd like that," she said as the bus arrived at school.

Heidi and Stanley stood up and filed off the bus with the other kids. Stanley met up with his friends.

Lucy Lancaster and Bruce waved Heidi over to the playground.

"Sorry you had to sit with Stanley," said Bruce. "I told that kid my seat was saved, but he wouldn't budge."

Heidi shrugged and said, "No biggie."

She decided to keep her secret about Stanley to herself.

Chapter 3

PANICKY PRINCIPAL

Heidi skipped down the hall to her classroom—until she heard Principal Pennypacker on the PA system.

"Attention, students! Attention, students!" he announced. "Will Heidi Heckelbeck and Melanie Maplethorpe please come to the principal's office?"

Lucy and Bruce looked at Heidi as if she had suddenly turned into a criminal.

"Heidi, what did you DO?!" asked Lucy.

Heidi's mind cartwheeled as she tried to think if she *had* done anything.

"Nothing that I know of," she said.

Then the principal came back on the PA system. *"Please HURRY, girls!"*

Lucy's and Bruce's eyes grew even wider.

"He sounds worried," said Bruce.

"Maybe even panicky," added Lucy.

Heidi tried to play it cool. "I'm sure everything's fine," she said, but her perfect-day feeling was beginning to slip.

Principal Pennypacker greeted Heidi at the door of his office. "Heidi, please come inside. Melanie is already here."

Heidi sat next to Melanie, who looked very bored.

"Okay. What's the deal, Principal Pennypacker?" asked Melanie. "Did we, like, win an award or something? Or are we changing schools because we're too smart for this place?"

Heidi rolled her eyes and thought, *Sometimes Melanie can be so rude!*

Principal Pennypacker slid his hands into his pockets. "No, no, it's nothing like that," he said. "I need to know if either of you have been having the *perfect day*."

Melanie's ponytail swished from side to side as she shook her head.

"I'm having an average day," she said. "It's fine, but not perfect."

The principal pressed his hands together. *"Good!"* he declared. "A plain old normal day is just right! And what about *you*, Heidi?"

"I actually AM having a PERFECT day," Heidi admitted. "Is that bad?"

The principal nervously patted the tuft of hair on either side of his head—maybe to make sure they were still there.

"Oh merg!" was all he said.

Suddenly a swirl of sparkles circled around Heidi, Melanie, and the principal.

Then—*whoosh!*—the sparkles swished right out the window.

Melanie sat up straight. "What just happened?"

Principal Pennypacker gave them a worried smile. "Oh, I'm sure it's nothing to worry about," he said.

"You two can go back to class now. I'll take it from here."

Melanie stood up. "I would just like to say, something super-weird just happened and now we have to go back to class. So this is officially NOT a perfect day."

And for the first time in her life, Heidi agreed with Melanie.

She had seen that swirl of sparkles before, and she knew exactly what it was: magic.

And all that magic had *left* the room. But did that mean Heidi's had left her, too?

Chapter 4

HICCUPS!

As the girls walked back to class, Heidi no longer had a spring in her step. She wanted the feeling of a perfect day to come back.

Well, at least I still have the lollipop Stanley gave me, she thought as she pulled out the candy.

"Oh, you shouldn't have, Heidi! You are SO sweet!" said Melanie as she snatched the sucker right out of Heidi's hand. "Eeeew, GROSS! It's GRAPE! No thanks."

Then Melanie flung the lollipop into a trash can. *Clunk!*

Heidi clenched her fists and said, "Melanie—that was MINE!"

Melanie shrugged. "Oops, I thought it was for me," she explained. "But I did you a FAVOR, Heidi. Grape lollipops are disgusting, and they turn your tongue PURPLE, like a lizard's! So . . . you're welcome."

With that, Melanie walked into the classroom. Heidi wanted to fish her lollipop out of the trash, but it was the trash can next to the boys' bathroom . . . which everyone called the "trash can of no return."

Heidi's perfect day kept going downhill. Lunch was fish sticks. School fish sticks were always mushy. And to make matters worse, everyone kept asking why she and Melanie had been called to the office.

Lucy plopped her lunch tray onto the table. "So, what happened in the office?" she asked. "There's a rumor that you and Melanie got in BIG trouble."

Heidi rolled her eyes.

"Principal Pennypacker just asked about our day," she said. "We're not in trouble."

"Well, that's a relief," said Lucy. Then she picked up a fish stick that was so soggy, it broke in half.

"Ew," said Lucy. "This is one squooshy fish stick! I wish we could have PIZZA instead."

Then Heidi's friend hiccupped, and the absolute weirdest thing happened. A trail of magical sparkles shivered from around Lucy and swooshed into the kitchen.

40

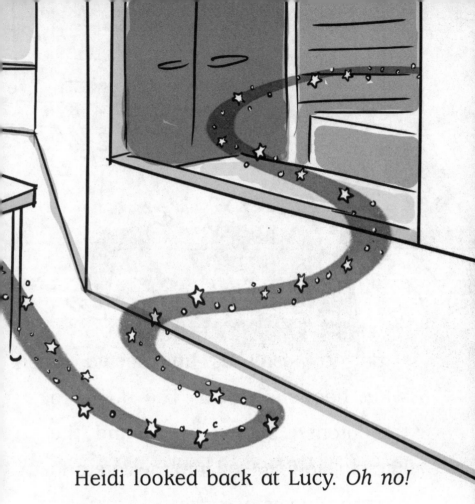

Heidi looked back at Lucy. *Oh no!*
What just happened?

Lucy covered her mouth and said,
"Excuse me! That was unexpected!"

But it wasn't as unexpected as what happened next. The doors to the kitchen swung open, and the kitchen staff walked into the cafeteria carrying boxes of *pizza*.

"Attention, students!" said the head cook. "Today you deserve something

better than fish sticks, so we're giving everyone *free* pizza!"

The kids burst into cheers—everyone except Heidi. Because Heidi had just seen magic come from her best friend. And her best friend wasn't even a witch!

WATCHDOG

Is my best friend MAGIC? Or was it my imagination? Heidi wondered.

Either way, Heidi decided to keep an eye on Lucy to see if she would hiccup again. Watchdog Heidi discovered Lucy did a lot of different things.

Lucy yawned. Lucy stretched. Lucy twirled her pencil. Lucy often pushed her glasses up the bridge of her nose. She also raised  her hand a lot, which reminded Heidi that her best friend was *really smart*.

The only thing Lucy *didn't* do was hiccup. No hiccups in math. No hiccups in science. Now they were in art, painting pottery bowls.

Mr. Doodlebee caught Heidi staring at Lucy.

"Heidi, keep your eyes on your own project," he said. "You don't need to watch what Lucy's doing."

Lucy looked at Heidi and giggled. Heidi blushed and tried to talk it off.

"Your bowl looks AMAZING, Lucy," she said.

And it was totally true. Lucy had painted the cutest daisies on her perfectly round bowl.

Heidi's bowl, on the other hand, was definitely *not* perfectly round. It was a little crooked and wobbly . . . and maybe not even a bowl?

Why doesn't my art ever turn out the way I think it will? she wondered.

"Could you please pass the pink paint, Heidi?" Lucy whispered.

Heidi slid the jar of pink paint across the table just a little too fast. *Zoop!*

The jar bumped into Lucy's bowl,
which slid off the table and onto the
floor. *SMASH!*

"My bowl!" Lucy cried. "It's . . .
Hiccup!"

Heidi gasped as a puff of magic
floated under the table.

There she goes AGAIN!

"Oh no!" said Mr. Doodlebee. "Lucy,
is your poor bowl okay? It was one of
the best-shaped bowls in the class!"

Lucy stood up from under the table and held up her still-perfect, very unbroken bowl.

"Yes!" she said. "Somehow it's MAGICALLY fine!"

Chapter 6

MAGICAL MAYHEM!

Oh no! Oh no! Oh no! Heidi thought on the bus home from school.

Stanley sat down beside her. Any other afternoon, Heidi would *love* sitting next to her *not-a-secret-anymore admirer.*

But not *this* afternoon.

"What's so 'Oh no!'?" Stanley asked.

Heidi looked hard at Stanley. "Wait, did I say 'Oh no!' out loud?"

Stanley thought for a moment. "You must have, or how else would I have heard you?"

Heidi nodded. But she sensed something weird was going on.

*At least I didn't mention what
happened with Lucy*, she thought.

"What happened with Lucy?"
Stanley asked.

Heidi looked at Stanley like he
was from another planet. *Oh my
gosh! Stanley must be READING MY
MIND!*

Stanley laughed and said, "Heidi, don't be silly. I can't read minds! That's impossible."

Heidi changed the subject quickly so Stanley wouldn't know that he was reading her mind. "So, how was your day?"

"Totally great!" he said. "Can you believe we got pizza instead of fish sticks? That was like real MAGIC!"

The word "magic" sent a cold chill over Heidi's entire body.

Luckily, the bus groaned to a stop at Heidi's corner.

"Well, gotta go!" she said. Heidi raced off the bus and ran all the way home.

"MOM!" she shouted as she came inside. "Meet me in the family room!"

Mom was already in the family room, reading a book.

"What's up?" she asked.

"Mom, can magic disappear?" Heidi asked. "I mean, like, go somewhere else?"

Mom set her book on her lap. "Only under certain circumstances, but it's very rare. *Why?*"

Before Heidi could answer, Aunt Trudy burst in the front door and charged into the family room.

"We have a magical emergency!" she shouted.

Heidi and Mom exchanged a glance.

Then a hiccup came from the kitchen.

"HELP!" Dad cried.
Heidi, Mom, and Aunt
Trudy rushed in to find their
dishes and silverware had gone
bananas!

Everything flew through the air all by itself! Even the pots and pans were cooking food . . . by themselves!

"All I did was hiccup, and *this* happened!" cried Dad.

Mom tried to stop the madness with magic, but her magic didn't work.

"Oh dear! *My* magic," said Mom.
"It's *gone*!"

Dad dodged a spatula. "Well, there
is certainly no lack of magic in our
kitchen!"

Aunt Trudy shook her car keys. "Come on!" she said. "We're going to the Magical Library to find answers!"

Then the girls bolted out the door and left Dad to fend for himself.

Chapter 7

THE PERFECTUS MALUS

The three witches flew into the Brewster Library on a mission.

They rushed to the secret magical section. Aunt Trudy held her library card in front of a portrait of an old librarian dressed like a wizard, and the wall opened.

65

But all was not well inside the Magical Library either. Books flew around like planes without a flight pattern. The covers flapped like bird wings. Ms. Egli, the head librarian, was trying to catch the books with a butterfly net.

"Come back here!" she cried, swatting left and right.

Then she noticed Aunt Trudy, Heidi, and Mom.

"Hello, ladies!" Ms. Egli cried. "Please grab a net and help me catch these wild books! There's magical mischief in the library today!"

So they grabbed nets and charged after the flying books. As soon as a book was caught, it quietly returned to its rightful place on the shelf.

One book was especially sneaky. Heidi chased after it around the tree that stood in the middle of the library.

But what she found on the other side of the tree was a familiar man who had a tuft of hair on either side of his head.

Heidi stopped in her tracks.

"Principal Pennypacker?! What are YOU doing here?!"

The principal looked up from the book he was studying.

"I am looking for an answer to our magical problem, and I think I've found it!" he said.

Ms. Egli, Aunt Trudy, and Mom put down their nets and ran over. The principal held up a book called *The Perfectus Malus*.

"That's the same book we came to look at!" Aunt Trudy cried.

Heidi couldn't believe what was happening. "Wait!" she interrupted. "Principal Pennypacker, are you MAGIC?"

"Well, not at the moment," the principal admitted. "I've lost my magic, due to the Perfectus Malus."

Heidi shook her head. "The WHAT?"

"The Perfectus Malus! It's a magical transfer that is very, very, very rare," Principal Pennypacker explained. "The transfer usually happens when the magic of a witch or a wizard latches on to someone or something close to them."

Ms. Egli put
her hands on her
hips. "Well, that explains the
wackiness in the library!" she cried.
"My magic must have gone to my
books!"

The principal nodded and continued. "Most witches and wizards don't notice it because the magic returns to them the next day. However, if someone else knowingly uses the magic during the Perfectus Malus, then the magic becomes confused and won't know where it belongs."

Uh-oh, thought Heidi. "Then what happens?"

Principal Pennypacker took off his glasses. "If the magic becomes confused between its true witch or wizard, the magic could go—*and*

stay—with someone *else*," he said.
"This means the rightful witch or
wizard could lose their magic *forever.*"

Heidi gulped. "FOREVER forever?"

The principal nodded. "Yes. Forever
forever."

Chapter 8

A MAGIC WITCH HUNT

"Let's not panic!" Ms. Egli said. "Try to think where your magic could've gone. Mine has clearly gone to these flying books, so order should be restored tomorrow."

"I'll bet my magic has gone to my husband!" said Mom.

"And my magic has either gone to my bird or to one of my two cats," said Aunt Trudy. "Hmm. There were a lot of pet treats floating around my house, now that I think about it!"

Heidi instantly knew where her magic had gone as well . . . to *Lucy*.

"Mom, can you take me to the Lancasters'?" Heidi asked.

"Of course," said Mom.

Then Aunt Trudy herded Heidi and Mom to the car and drove them to Lucy's house.

Mrs. Lancaster answered the door.

"Is Lucy home?" asked Heidi. "I need to talk to her about the most important thing EVER!"

"Hi, Heidi! Lucy is at Stanley's house," said Mrs. Lancaster. "It's right down the street."

Heidi turned to Mom and asked, "Can I go?"

Mom nodded, and Heidi took off like a rocket. She sped by three houses and then spied Lucy and Stanley playing Hacky Sack in the Stonewreckers' front yard. They saw Heidi too.

"Hey, Heidi! Wanna play Hacky Sack with us?" called Stanley. "We're getting really good! We just did a hundred kicks in a row!"

Heidi tried to catch her breath. "Actually, I need to talk to Lucy. . . ."

But Stanley had already kicked the Hacky Sack. Lucy toe-kicked the sack to Heidi and hiccupped.

Poof! A flurry of magic sparkles surrounded the Hacky Sack as it flew.

Oh no! thought Heidi.

Acting quickly, she whomped the sack as hard as she could so that no one could see the magic.

ZOOOOOOOOOM!

The sack flew right over Stanley's house!

Stanley watched it soar away. "Wow!" he cheered. "What a STRIKE, Heidi! I've never seen anything like it!"

Heidi laughed nervously. "I must be stronger than I think!"

"I'll get it," said Stanley.

He ran off to find the Hacky Sack, which meant Heidi and Lucy were finally alone.

"Lucy, I REALLY need to talk with you!" Heidi said.

Lucy waved both hands at Heidi.

"No, no, Heidi!" she said. "I need to talk to YOU first! PLEASE let me go FIRST!"

Then Lucy leaned in close and whispered in her best friend's ear. "Heidi, I think I'm MAGIC."

Chapter 9

THE MOMENT OF TRUTH

Lucy couldn't stop talking.

"Just think about it, Heidi! I wished for pizza at lunch, and we got PIZZA! And when my bowl smashed in art, I wished it hadn't happened, and my bowl was okay! There's no other way to explain it! I MUST be MAGIC!"

Heidi took a deep breath. Well, here it was. The moment of truth. The moment she had feared since the day she found out she was a witch: Heidi had to share her secret.

"It's not YOU, Lucy," said Heidi. "The magic is MINE. Well, it USED to be mine. Oh, Lucy! I have a secret, and you can't tell ANYONE. . . . *I'm a WITCH!*"

"WHAT?!" exclaimed Lucy in disbelief. "You're a WITCH? But how? Witches are ugly and old with pointy hats and cauldrons and spells with eyes of newts. And, um, do you have a black cat?"

Heidi rolled her eyes and explained, "No, silly! Those are all STORYBOOK witch things.

I'm a REAL witch, and real witches look like normal people, except they're magic. Well, that is, until the Perfectus Malus happened."

Lucy gasped. "The Perfectus Malus? Wow, that sounds BAD."

"It IS bad," said Heidi. "It transfers a witch's magic to someone else. In my case, it was YOU, and maybe a little bit Stanley."

"But I would never take your magic away, Heidi!" Lucy said. "Can I wish it BACK to you?!"

Lucy shut her eyes and was about to wish the magic back to Heidi. But Heidi grabbed her friend by the arm.

"NO! STOP!" she whisper-shouted. "The magic will come back to me BY ITSELF as long as you don't use it ON PURPOSE. The pizza, the unbroken bowl, and even the Hacky Sack were all you using the magic without knowing it. If you use the magic on purpose, the magic will get confused and may not come back to me. Ever."

Lucy nodded. "So if I wish the magic BACK to you, I would be using it on purpose and that's not good. Okay, I promise not to use the magic on purpose!"

Heidi threw her arms around Lucy. "Oh my gosh, thank you, Lucy!" she said.

Lucy pulled back and looked into Heidi's eyes. "I still can't believe you're a WITCH," she said. "We'll have to talk about this more tomorrow."

Heidi could hear Stanley running back toward them. He was holding up the Hacky Sack in victory.

"You really walloped that sack, Heidi!" Stanley said. "It went into the yard BEHIND my backyard! You've got some MAGIC foot there!"

Heidi looked at her foot and then back at Lucy. Then they both fell over laughing.

Chapter 10

BEWiTCHED

The next morning Heidi heard moaning and wailing in her room.

"*WOOOOOO! WOOOOOO!*"

It was a *ghost*! A real ghost was floating in her room!

Heidi screamed and pulled the covers over her head.

Then she heard giggles. *Henry's* giggles. She pulled down the covers. Henry yanked a sheet off his body.

"GOTCHA!" he said. "Now get up! Or you'll miss the bus!"

Heidi kicked off her covers.

"Merg," she grumbled. This was definitely *not* the start of a perfect day. This was the start of a normal day. Maybe that was a good sign?

Heidi slid out of bed and hurried to the kitchen.

"Mom, did you get your magic back?" she asked.

Mom gave a snap to answer, and there was a puff of smoke. Instantly Heidi was changed out of her pajamas and dressed for school with a full breakfast in front of her.

"Does that answer your question?" Mom said with a wink. "And I sense your magic is back too."

As soon as Mom said this, a whoosh of warmth flowed through Heidi's body. Her magic was back!

"Welcome back, old friend," she whispered.

On the bus Heidi noticed neither Bruce nor Stanley was there. She was actually kind of glad, because her worries weren't over yet. Heidi still had to face Lucy. What would life be like now that Lucy knew she was magic?

As usual, Lucy was waiting for her when the bus pulled in. "We have to talk," said Lucy the moment Heidi's feet hit the ground.

Heidi braced herself for the witch conversation. *Here it comes!* she thought. *The talk I never wanted to have.*

Lucy grabbed Heidi by the hand and pulled her away from the other kids.

"So FYI, Bruce's mom called MY mom and said Bruce wouldn't be on the bus today," Lucy said. "But you probably already noticed that."

Heidi raised an eyebrow. "So you think I noticed because I'M MAGIC?"

Lucy laughed. "No, silly, I think you noticed because you were ON THE BUS," she said. "Why would I think you're MAGIC?"

Heidi's backpack slid right off her shoulder and crashed onto the ground.

What in all of Brewster is going on? Heidi thought.

Before Heidi could say anything, Principal Pennypacker walked over.

"Just the student I was looking for!" he said. "Lucy, may I borrow Heidi for a moment?"

Lucy nodded and said, "Of course! See you in class, Heidi."

Heidi waved as her friend left, and then she turned to the principal.

"I told Lucy I was MAGIC yesterday, but she doesn't seem to remember any of it now," Heidi said. "How is that possible?"

The principal smiled. "Good," he said. "Apparently anyone affected by the Perfectus Malus forgets everything that happened to them once the magic transfers back."

Heidi clapped her hands. That meant Stanley would forget about reading her mind too.

"Best news EVER!" Heidi said with a squeal, even though she was not a squealy kid.

"It's called The Forgetting," said Principal Pennypacker. "Soon you won't remember that I'm magic either, which is why I want to give you this."

He pulled a booklet from his pocket and handed it to Heidi. It said *Broomsfield Academy* across the top.

"This is some information about a boarding school that also has a secret School of Magic," he said. "Maybe you'd like to apply when you're old enough?"

"Yes, sir, I'd love that!" said Heidi. "My friend Sunny mentioned this school to me. I can't wait to learn more! Thank you!"

The principal nodded. "Your mother and Aunt Trudy can tell you more about it too," he said. "Now off to class, or you'll be late!"

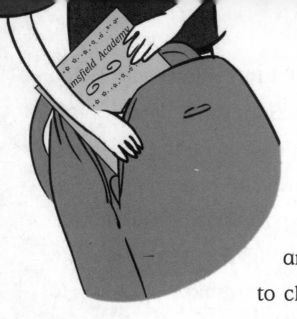

Heidi shoved the booklet into her backpack and headed to class.

Lucy was waiting at the desk next to hers. She was fidgeting with a mechanical pencil.

"What did Principal Pennypacker want NOW?" she asked.

"Oh, nothing," said Heidi. "He just wanted to give me some school booklet."

Lucy nodded and twisted her mechanical pencil again. It still didn't work.

"Do you have a pencil I can borrow?" she asked. "Mine's broken."

"Let me check," said Heidi. She leaned over and rummaged through her backpack for her pencil case.

Hiccup!

Heidi paused and felt a sizzle of magic in the air . . . but then she shook it off.

"Hey, did you just hiccup?" Heidi asked Lucy.

"Uh, yeah, I guess I did," said Lucy.

"Weird. Well, here you go," said Heidi as she handed Lucy a purple pencil.

Her friend smiled. "Actually, never mind! Mine's working again! Thanks anyway!"

Heidi shrugged and popped the pencil back into her case and sighed. *Well, it sure is nice to have everything back to normal again.*

There's more

HE:D: HECKELBECK

to explore!

HEiDi HECKELBECK Is Not a Thief!

HEiDi HECKELBECK Says Cheese!

HEiDi HECKELBECK Might Be Afraid of the Dark

HEiDi HECKELBECK Is the Bestest Babysitter!

HEiDi HECKELBECK Makes a Wish SUPER SPECIAL!

HEiDi HECKELBECK and the Big Mix-Up

HEiDi HECKELBECK Tries Out for the Team

HEiDi HECKELBECK and the Magic Puppy

HEiDi HECKELBECK and the Never-Ending Day

HEiDi HECKELBECK Has a New Best Friend

HEiDi HECKELBECK and the Snoopy Spy

HEiDi HECKELBECK Is So Totally Grounded!

HEiDi HECKELBECK Lights! Camera! Awesome!

HEiDi HECKELBECK Lends a Helping Hand

HEiDi HECKELBECK and the Wacky Tacky Spirit Week

HEiDi HECKELBECK Takes the Cake

HEiDi HECKELBECK Pool Party!

HEiDi HECKELBECK for Class President!

HEiDi HECKELBECK and the Hair Emergency!

HEiDi HECKELBECK and the Lost Library Book

HEiDi HECKELBECK and the Snow Day Surprise

HEiDi HECKELBECK Sunshine Magic

Have you ever wondered what Heidi Heckelbeck's life is like when she grows up? You don't need magic to find out! Introducing